AMOS
CAMPS OUT

A COUCH ADVENTURE
IN THE WOODS

by SUSAN SELIGSON
and HOWIE SCHNEIDER

JOY STREET BOOKS

Little, Brown and Company
Boston   Toronto   London

For Sarah, Alyce, Benjamin, C.J., and Samuel

Copyright © 1992 by Howie Schneider
and Susan Seligson

First Edition

Library of Congress Cataloging-in-Publication Data

Seligson, Susan.
    Amos camps out : a couch adventure in the woods / by Susan Seligson
and Howie Schneider. — 1st ed.
        p.   cm.
    Summary: Amos, the dog who travels by motorized couch, discovers
the joys and tribulations of camping.
    ISBN 0-316-77402-2
    [1. Dogs—Fiction.   2. Furniture—Fiction.   3. Camping—Fiction.]
I. Schneider, Howie, 1930–   II. Title.
PZ7.S456946A1zj   1992
[E]—dc20   91-45305

    Joy Street Books are published by Little, Brown and Company (Inc.)

            10 9 8 7 6 5 4 3 2 1

                    WOR

            Published simultaneously in Canada
        by Little, Brown & Company (Canada) Limited

        Printed in the United States of America

Amos is an old dog who spends almost all his time on the couch.

But that doesn't mean
he spends all his time at home.

Ever since he discovered he
could make his couch MOVE,
Amos goes nearly everywhere
he wants to go.

VAROOM...

Amos loves to visit his friends all around the neighborhood.

He knows all the streets and sidewalks, so no matter where he goes he always finds his way home.

Mr. and Mrs. Bobson take Amos lots of places. But Amos has never been on a camping trip. One day the Bobsons decided to take him on one. They packed a lot of strange bundles.

"You're going to love camping," Mrs. Bobson said. "The woods are full of wonderful new smells and creatures."

Amos could hardly wait.

Early the next morning the Bobsons loaded up the car. "Hooray!" thought Amos. "They're taking my hot dogs!"

Soon they were on their way.

After a few hours, they arrived at the campground.
"Welcome, folks," said the park ranger. "A couch! I can see
you sure like to be comfortable."

"Oh, the couch isn't for us," said Mr. Bobson.
"It's for our dog, Amos."

When they got to the campsite, Mrs. Bobson said, "Isn't this a wonderful spot?"

Amos looked around. "Wonderful? There's nothing here but trees," he thought.

"Let's eat!" said Mr. Bobson.

He went to collect some firewood.

Amos tried to help.

He collected some other things, too!

Soon Amos smelled his favorite supper: hot dogs!
He was so hungry he didn't even mind sharing them with the ants.

After dinner Amos grew sleepy.
He wondered when they were
going home.

But just then, Mrs. Bobson called, "Time for bed," and showed
Amos his tent.

"I have to sleep in *there?*" wondered
Amos. "How will I fit?" He inched
his couch inside as far as it would go.

"Good night, Amos!"
said the Bobsons.

But it wasn't a good night. Amos didn't sleep at all.
It was cold and scary, and mosquitoes buzzed around him all
night long.

The next morning after breakfast the park ranger drove by.
"You'd better lock your food up tight, folks," he called.
"There are lots of hungry wild animals around. We've seen
their tracks."
"Thanks," said Mr. Bobson. "We'll be careful."

The Bobsons washed the breakfast dishes and locked the food up tight. "Let's go fishing," said Mr. Bobson. They grabbed the fishing gear and started down toward the stream.

Amos tried to follow close behind.

But it wasn't easy. Soon Amos grew tired and thirsty. He decided to stop for a drink.

Suddenly Amos couldn't see the Bobsons anywhere.
"Hey, which way did they go?" he wondered. "How does
anyone know his way around here without any sidewalks or
streets?"

Just when he feared he was lost,
Amos spotted the Bobsons up ahead.

They all spent an exciting afternoon fishing.
"This is more like it," Amos thought.

When they got back to the campsite, Amos spied someone sniffing the food box.

"My hot dogs!" Amos thought.

"AMOS!" shouted Mrs. Bobson. "Watch out! That's a skunk!"

"Whew. I nearly lost my hot dogs," thought Amos.
"And it's almost suppertime, too!"

"Amos!" Mrs. Bobson called. "Look what we're having for dinner!"
"Fish?" thought Amos. "Yuck! Fish is for cats!"

After dinner they all sat under the stars and sang their favorite songs.

Soon it was time for bed.

They all settled into their tents.
Even Amos fell fast asleep.

Suddenly Amos heard noises right outside his tent.
Scratch, scratch, scratch. "What's out there?" he wondered.
"Whatever it is, it's very close."

SCRATCH
SCRATCH
SCRATCH

When he worked up the courage to peek outside, he could
hardly believe his eyes. His hot dogs were disappearing into
the woods!

"Hey, come back!" he yelped. "Those are mine!"
He revved up his couch and shot out of his tent.

In minutes he found himself deep in the woods. There was no
sign of the thief or the hot dogs.

Then he heard something familiar.
Chomp, chomp. And he smelled a familiar smell.

"MY HOT DOGS!"
he thought.

Amos raced over. He bit down and tugged. But the hot dogs
wouldn't budge. So he threw his couch into reverse and
pulled as hard as he could.

Suddenly there was a loud SNAP.

And Amos found himself staring at the thief . . .

... but not for long.

"Boy, that was close," he thought. "I'd better get back to the campsite now. What if the Bobsons wake up and find me gone?"

"But which way is the campsite?" he wondered.

"*This* way?"

"No, it must be *that* way."

"Or is it *this* way?"

"Or *that* way?"

Amos realized he was completely lost.
"How will I ever find it?" he worried.
"This is scary. I wish I were safe in my
own little tent now."

Amos didn't know what to do.
So he munched on his hot dogs until
his belly was full. Then he fell asleep
right there in the woods.

When Amos woke up, the sun was shining, the birds were singing, and the woods smelled wonderful. Now that it wasn't dark anymore, Amos realized there was nothing to be afraid of. In fact, it was *nice*.

But he was still lost.

Then he noticed something he couldn't have seen in the dark: tracks. Not animal tracks—COUCH tracks!

"All I have to do is follow my tracks and I'll be back in no time,"
thought Amos. Happily he set off for the campsite.
On the way he had some fun . . .

making new friends . . .

and visiting old ones.

Back at the campsite, Amos was relieved to find the Bobsons still asleep. "It feels great to be back in my own tent," he thought as he slipped quietly inside.

When the Bobsons awoke, they saw the overturned food box. "A wild animal was here last night," called Mr. Bobson. "Well, he must have been a very *quiet* wild animal," said Mrs. Bobson. "He didn't even wake Amos."

Soon people from the neighboring campsites gathered around.
"There was an animal in our campsite, too," said one.
"It must have been a bear," said another.
"Luckily the ranger scared him away!"

"Not me," said the ranger as he drove up.
"I was in my cabin the whole night long."
"But we heard a motor," the campers said.

"Well, who could it have been?" asked Mrs. Bobson.

Just then Amos woke up. **VAROOM**

"*That's* what we heard!" everyone said.
"Say, you don't suppose . . ." said the ranger.
"It was our Amos!" cried Mrs. Bobson. "*You* scared the bear away!" "What a brave dog!" said Mr. Bobson.

"We could sure use *you* around here, Amos," said the ranger.

Soon it was time to head home. Everyone said good-bye, and the Bobsons loaded Amos's couch onto the car.

"What a wonderful trip," said Mrs. Bobson. "We just knew you would love camping, Amos!"

They were right.
In fact, he liked it so
much that from then on,
Amos camped out . . .

...whenever he wanted.